THE DJANGO

This book belongs to:

....

For Ma and Pa — L.P.

A TEMPLAR BOOK

First published in the UK in 2010 by Templar Publishing.
This softback edition published in the UK in 2011 by
Templar Publishing, an imprint of The Templar Company Limited,
Deepdene Lodge, Deepdene Avenue, Dorking, Surrey, RH5 4AT, UK
www.templarco.co.uk

Copyright © 2010 by Levi Pinfold

3 5 7 9 10 8 6 4

ISBN 978-1-84877-101-7

Printed in China

THE
DJANGO
LEVI PINFOLD

templar publishing
www.templarco.co.uk

(O)nce, I met a Django.

A what?

A Django. It's like a thing. A sort of *it*. A kind of *cozzler* that can easily find trouble.

It was standing inside our home one day, staring at Papa's banjo and saying, "Cor, lovely!"

When I went in it saw me.

"Hello," it said.

"Hello," I said back.

"I like that shiny thing," it said, pointing to the banjo.

"So do I, but it's Papa's and NOBODY is allowed to touch it," I warned.

"Well! Fancy! I'm just that — a true to life N-O-B-O-D-Y. It's only my blooming middle name," it said, as it started to twang the strings.

I said, "Don't!" but it ignored me. Then it started to prance around and sing.

As it sang,

it twanged the strings.

And as they twanged,

something crackled
and crunched.

Then came a smunch,

a swoosh...
and scrunch.

Then a huge whack

and a massive SNAP!

And all of a sudden, Papa's banjo was dead.

"Ho-*ho!*" ho-hoed the Django. "That was fun! Have
you got another one?"

"Of course not!" I shouted. "Look what you've done."

In a few moments, Papa arrived, yelling, "What's all
this noise? What's the hoo-ha about?"

He saw the smashed up thing, then looked at me.

I said, "Yes," and he said, "What?" and I said, "It was that
thing that did it!" pointing to where the Django should be.

"There's NOBODY there!" he yelled.

"I know!" I shouted.

"Right. You're going to bed and you're not to have
a spot of dinner!" cried Papa.

Oh, that made me huff – I hadn't done a thing!

But that was how the Django got in.

Papa was still as mad as an ape the next morning,
I'll tell you that.

He told me I was to work to earn the money for
a new banjo, starting with fetching some water for Wilfred
the old horse. So off I went, through the trees and
down to the waterside. When I got there I started to
fill up my pail.

"Hello," said a voice behind me.

"Not you again! Can't you go away?" I cried.

"Not likely," the Django said. "I'm always about.
What are we doing today?"

"Well, *I'm* doing extra chores because of *you*,"
I snapped and stomped off with the full
water pail.

I went a loopy way back to the camp,
a real screwy path, and I thought I'd lost the
horrible little rotter when I got back.

I was wrong.

As I carried the pail to Wilfred, that tricksy little Django's face popped out. Before I could jump, it opened its gob. Before I could move, out blurted a shout – an almighty ear-scrunching yell. A monstrous, massive, "GOBBLE-O-GOBBLE-O!"

Poor old Wilfred clearly didn't know what to think, so he reared up on his hind legs and ran for it.

It took ages for everybody to find him and calm him down, and guess who got the blame? ME.

Certainly not that thug, that scallywag, Django!

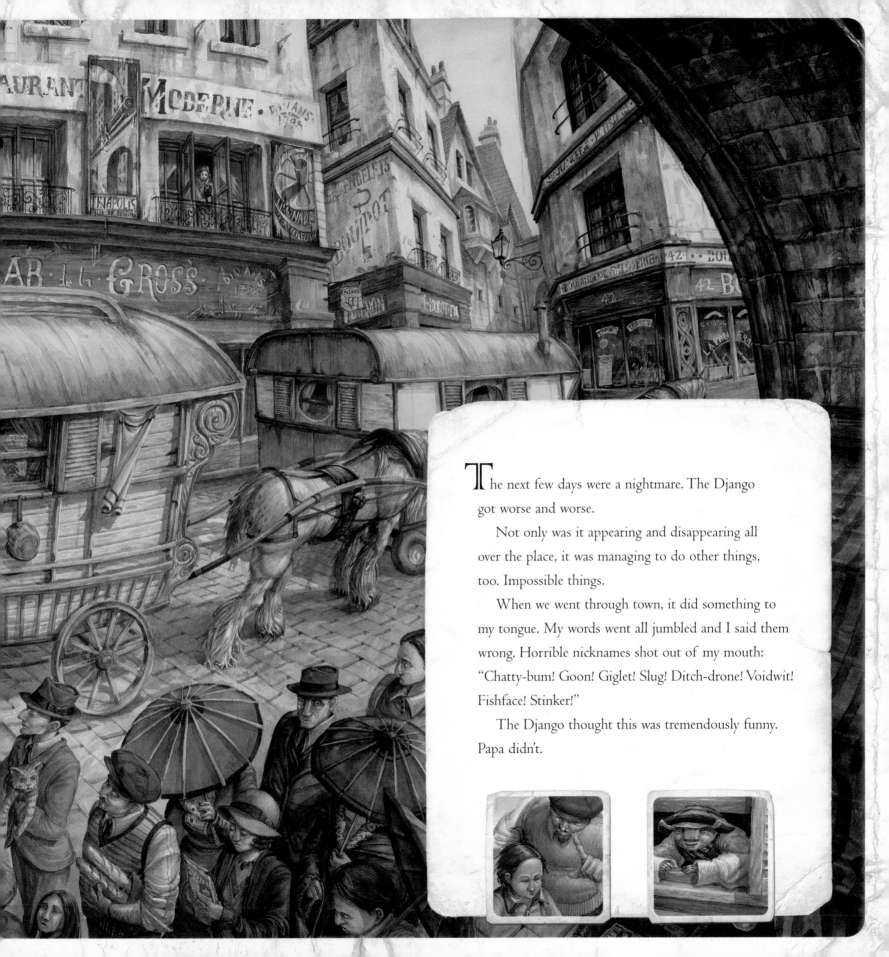

The next few days were a nightmare. The Django got worse and worse.

Not only was it appearing and disappearing all over the place, it was managing to do other things, too. Impossible things.

When we went through town, it did something to my tongue. My words went all jumbled and I said them wrong. Horrible nicknames shot out of my mouth: "Chatty-bum! Goon! Giglet! Slug! Ditch-drone! Voidwit! Fishface! Stinker!"

The Django thought this was tremendously funny. Papa didn't.

The day after that, we moved on.

I was told to sit extremely still so I'd not do any more mischief.

I tried.

At about midday we approached a farmhouse. All was calm. That was until I heard that familiar little, "Ho-*ho*!"

In a jot, my feet were dancing without my saying so and before I could work out what was happening I was hopping away from the caravan.

That blasted Django was getting into my legs now, too! I jigged my way into the pigsty, toe-tapped on the tractor, hoofed it in the cow field, and got down with the geese!

What a palaver. Now I had both a cross farmer and a *fuming* Papa on my hands.

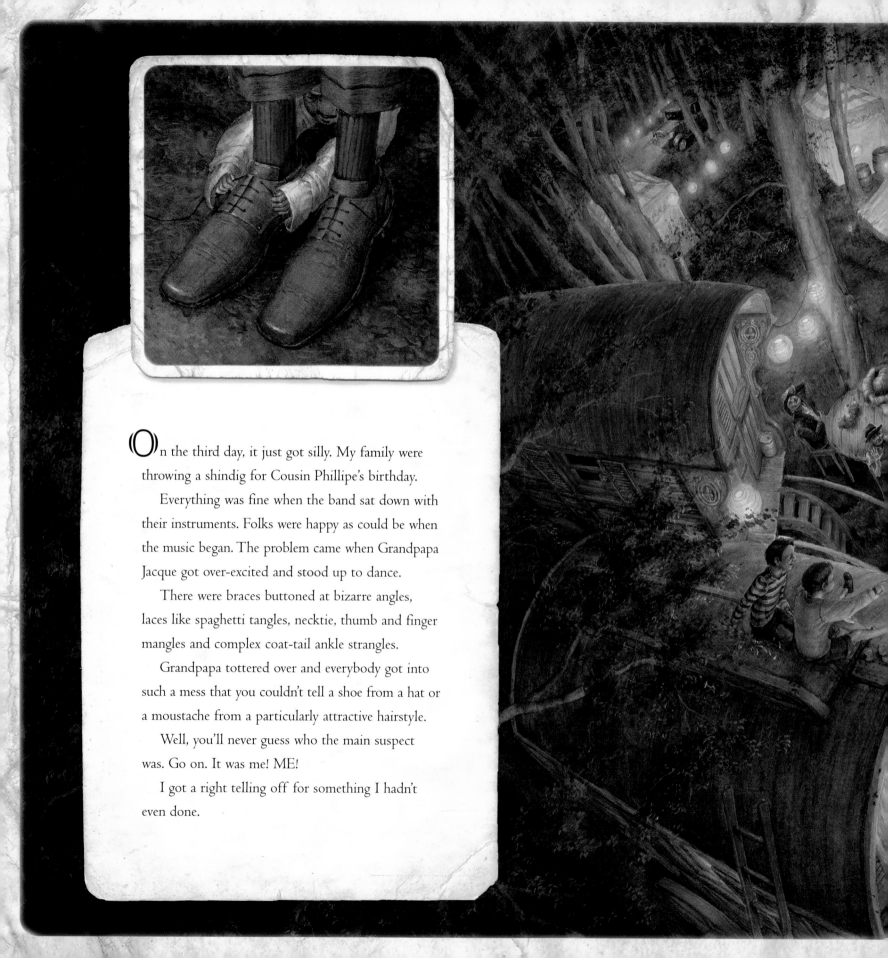

(O)n the third day, it just got silly. My family were throwing a shindig for Cousin Phillipe's birthday.

Everything was fine when the band sat down with their instruments. Folks were happy as could be when the music began. The problem came when Grandpapa Jacque got over-excited and stood up to dance.

There were braces buttoned at bizarre angles, laces like spaghetti tangles, necktie, thumb and finger mangles and complex coat-tail ankle strangles.

Grandpapa tottered over and everybody got into such a mess that you couldn't tell a shoe from a hat or a moustache from a particularly attractive hairstyle.

Well, you'll never guess who the main suspect was. Go on. It was me! ME!

I got a right telling off for something I hadn't even done.

I was sent straight to bed.

The Django was hiding in there when I arrived, chuckling. That was it. I exploded.

"You rotten peanut! You squirt! You spoofing little weasel-o! Can't you understand? I don't like your jokes. NOBODY likes your jokes. You don't belong here. GO SOMEWHERE ELSE!"

There was a silence. The Django had stopped its chuckling.

There was more silence, and then a very small voice came from under the sheets, "But... where would I go?" it said.

"I don't know! Wherever you went before!" I screeched. "JUST GO AWAY AND LEAVE ME ALONE!"

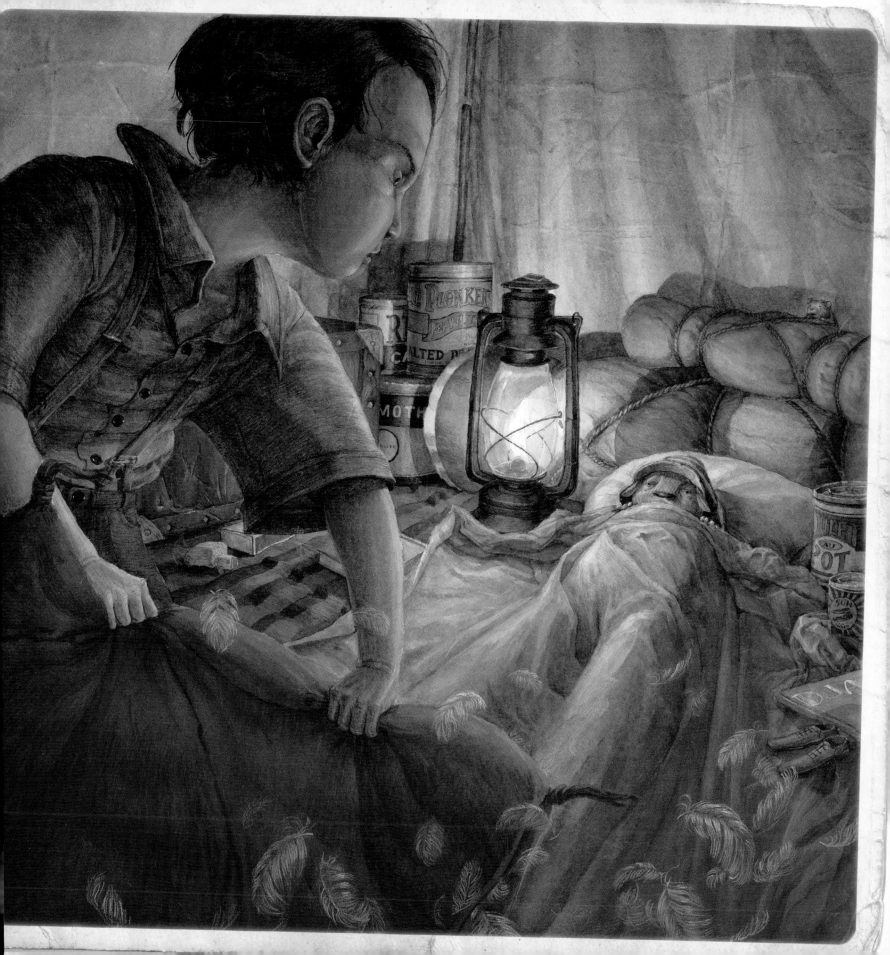

So it did.

I woke up the next morning expecting something to to happen.

I waited for a "Hello," as I ate my breakfast...

I waited for a "Ho-*ho!*" when I did my chores...

I waited for a "GOBBLE-O! GOBBLE-O!"
as I fed Wilfred…

By the time supper came around I was ready
for a *disaster*. But nothing happened. At all.

At the end of the week, Papa said, "What's wrong little Jean? You're as sad as a pike."

"Nothing," I said. "It's just that... oh... never mind. It's silly."

"Nonsense – you look as if someone's stolen all your marbles. What's making you act like a trodden-on bean, little man?"

"Well... you know the Django?"

"Oh, him," said Papa.

"I... I shouted and it went... and... I think I quite liked it really. I feel bad that I hurt it's feelings, but now it won't come back for me to say sorry."

"Oh dear. That Django's giving you the blues eh? Well, I think I've got something that might help to fix that," said Papa, swinging a rough bag down from his shoulder.

Out of it came a big something, wrapped tightly in layers of newspaper.

"Go on," said Papa. "Open it – it's yours."

Inside was a lovely, shiny banjo, looking better than new.

"I was going to give you mine, when I thought you were ready, but this one will have to do," said Papa. "Remember, a banjo is much more fun when you can play it, so take care of it."

"I will! I promise!" I said.

"Go ahead and pluck a string. It won't learn to play itself!"

I agreed and twanged a string. All of a sudden I felt a little bit better.

"Now pluck this one, with your finger on that spot there," said Papa.

I really liked the way it sounded when I did that.

"Cor! Thanks!" I said.

"That's all right," said Papa.

He sat with me for hours, helping me to make a tune with plenty of 'ho-hos' in. We even made up the words.

They went:

Ho, ho, oh, GOBBLE-O
NOBODY's there.
If a Django's the trouble-o,
you'd better beware!

Every time I sing it loudly enough, a very strange
thing happens...

I swear I can hear the tap-tap of small dancing
shoes and the sound of a small voice ho-*ho*-ing
along with me.

But when I turn to look, there's nobody there.

Whan, you don't believe me?
Well, try singing it yourself
and then you might hear it too.

THE REAL
DJANGO

This book is partly inspired by Django Reinhardt. If you already know who he is, you won't have to read any further. If not, this is what he looks like:

"What an elegant moustache!" I hear you cry and you're right. But this man wasn't simply a master of the moustache scissors; he was also a very talented jazz musician.

Django Reinhardt was born on 23rd January 1910. His mother was a French-speaking Romany and Django grew up surrounded by this unique culture.

Like little Jean in this book, Django loved music from a very young age. This led him to learn the violin and, as he grew older, the banjo and the guitar. Practising in every spare moment, Django became so skilled that by the time he was thirteen he had begun performing on stage. When he was eighteen, he was recorded playing the banjo and the recording was released as a record.

But just as everything seemed to be going so well for the young musician, a tragic accident happened: a fire began in the caravan he shared with his wife and Django was badly burned. His right leg was paralysed and the third and fourth fingers of his left hand were left almost unusable. It was thought he would never play the guitar again.

Then Django surprised everyone: within a year he was walking, but even more startling was his determination to play again. By practising tirelessly, he taught himself how to play with just two fingers. He was soon performing once more and rapidly turned his rotten luck around completely by forming the Quintette du Hot Club de France with violinist Stéphane Grappelli. Driven by Django's matchless playing, they are widely considered to have been one of the greatest European jazz bands in history.